RAINBOW FISH
THE DANGEROUS DEEP

Text by Leslie Goldman

Illustrations by Benrei Huang

 HarperFestival®

A Division of HarperCollins*Publishers*

One morning, Miss Cuttle called
her school of fish to order.
"Old Nemo will be here soon
to tell us all about his days
as a famous explorer," she said.

"Hooray!" Rainbow Fish cheered.
"Old Nemo tells great stories."
"The one about the giant jellyfish
is the best," said Spike.

"It is one of my favorites, too,"

added Old Nemo.

He told stories all morning.

After Old Nemo left,

Miss Cuttle had a hard time

getting her class back to work.

They did not want to sort shells.

They wanted to fight off giant jellyfish

and find secret caverns.

Miss Cuttle could see that
her class needed a break.
"I think you are all still off
in one of Old Nemo's stories.
Let's take an early recess."

After Old Nemo's tales of the sea,
recess at the Sunken Ship was not
very exciting.

"We can pretend we are brave
explorers," said Angel.

"I have a better idea," said Spike.

"Let's explore the reef."

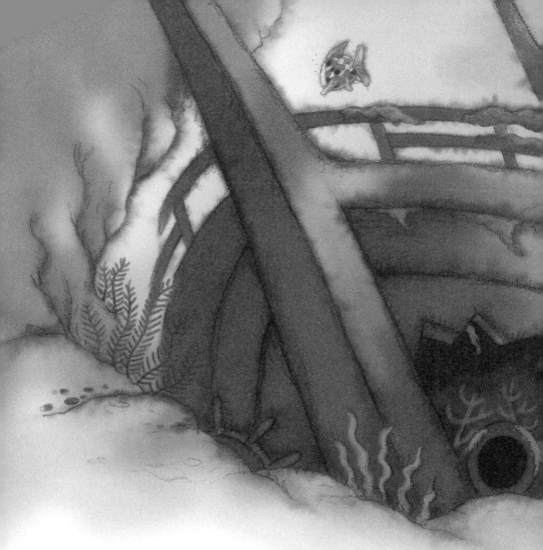

"That is a great idea," agreed
Rainbow Fish.
"But what will Miss Cuttle say?"
asked Angel.

"We will be back before she
even knows that we are gone,"
said Spike.

"Come on, follow me!"

Rainbow Fish, Spike, and Angel
jetted off toward the Oyster Beds.
"We can find a pearl just like Puffer did,"
Rainbow Fish said.

"It is not a real adventure
if someone has already done it,"
said Spike.

"What about the Crystal Caverns?"

asked Rainbow Fish.

"Ooh, they are so sparkly," added Angel.

"We have been there, too," said Spike.

"Old Nemo found them long ago."

"Do you have any better ideas?"

asked Rainbow Fish.

"We can go to the volcano," said Spike.

"No one *ever* goes there."

Off they went.

Spike stopped at the edge
of the volcano.

"I dare you to take a closer look."

"But we are not allowed to,"
said Rainbow Fish.
"Don't be such a scaredy-catfish,"
said Spike.

21

Suddenly a dark shadow appeared.

As it moved closer, it grew bigger.

The fish were frozen with fear.

"We should have stayed at school,"

whispered Angel.

A loud voice boomed from the
shadow.
"Does Miss Cuttle know where
you are?"

It was Old Nemo.

"I am so glad it is you, Old Nemo,"
said Rainbow Fish.

"We were really scared."

"There is much to be afraid of
in the deep," said Old Nemo.
"You young fish are very lucky.
The ocean deep is no place
for you."

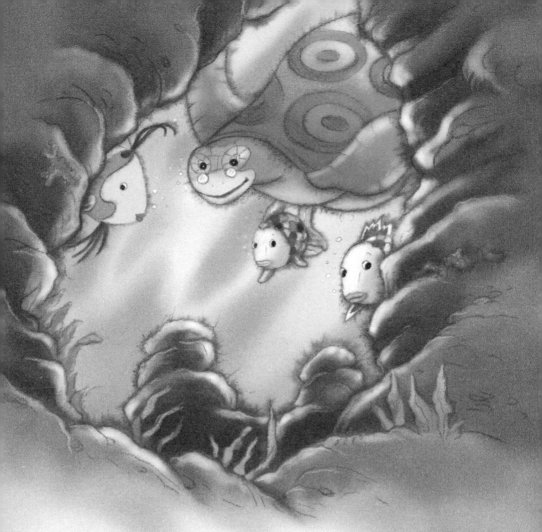

"We want to be brave
explorers," they said all at once.
"Many young fish dream about
the adventures that await them
in the deep," said Old Nemo.

"School is adventure enough

for young fish," said Old Nemo.

"You still have much to learn
before you will be ready to explore
the great beyond."
And with that, Old Nemo led them
back to Miss Cuttle's school.

Rainbow Fish, Spike, and Angel
told Miss Cuttle they were sorry
for swimming off by themselves.
They promised never to do it again.
"I am just glad you are back safe
and sound," she replied.

Old Nemo was right.

School was the only adventure

they needed.